D0396304

BE NOT
AFRAID

Alyssa Cole

BE NOT AFRAID
Copyright © 2016 Alyssa Cole

ALL RIGHTS RESERVED.

No part of this book may be reproduced or transmitted in any form or by any means, including electronic or photographic reproduction, in whole or in part, without express written permission, except in the case of brief passages embodied in critical reviews and articles.

BOOKS BY ALYSSA COLE

"Nevertheless, to the persecution and tyranny of his cruel ministry we will not tamely submit — appealing to Heaven for the justice of our cause, we determine to die or be free."

- JOSEPH WARREN

CHAPTER 1

August 1776
Brooklyn, New York

BE NOT AFRAID.

Elijah repeated the words to himself as he squatted in the marshy ditch — what was originally a battle cry now a command he forced himself to obey. The man who'd first shouted the words and charged the Redcoats at Boston Common had been courageous, but Elijah didn't plan on joining him in the ranks of dead Patriot Negroes quite yet. He had come close to it that night, though, despite his intentions.

He gripped the cold metal barrel of his Brown Bess with one hand. With the other, he pulled out a grimy handkerchief and wiped the blood from the bayonet. The Redcoat crumpled on the ground beside him had gasped his last breath only a moment before.

Elijah held no personal hatred for the Brits; he hadn't pulled away when the ruddy-cheeked man reached for him, fear and desperation in his eyes as his guts spilled out. Elijah had even said a quick prayer over the still-warm body before searching it for ammunition and rations. He had no qualms about the act — the Continental Army was poorly supplied and the lobsterbacks were funded by the Crown. Besides, the body-breaking labor men like him had been born into helped line the royal coffers. The petty theft could be seen as back pay, if one looked at things a certain way. Elijah wasn't sure that was the right mentality; the only thing he knew to be true was that he needed to be free and no man, Brit or Colonist, was going to obstruct his path now that it was a possibility.

Then why did you run?

Elijah shivered. The late summer night was unseasonably chill, and the wind cut through his shabby uniform, pieced together with other men's cast-offs, with ease. His breeches had ripped during his flight from the battle, and the cool air gained entrance there as well. He pulled at his ill-fitting jacket, too small to button at the front, and wished he were back at Sutton Farm tending to the horses and their animal warmth. Working with them was the only thing that made him feel at peace.

He shook his head at the indulgent thought.

Back at Sutton Farm you're a slave, and if you don't keep fighting you'll remain one, Elijah chided himself. He needed to stop reminiscing and find his regiment — what remained of them.

The attack on Brooklyn had been expected, given the area's sparse population, but it still caught the Continentals unawares. When the skirmish had started, for one shining moment Elijah thought they might take the day. Then the Brits had fallen upon them like a wave crashing into the shore, scattering the untrained American soldiers like so many particles of sand. One Patriot turned tail, and then another, and then fight turned to flight en masse as they sought escape from the onslaught of red-coated Regulars. Elijah had been filled with shame as he fled the skirmish, stumbling over the marshy land for who knew how long, but the emotion disappeared when he fell into a ditch and a British soldier tumbled in after him.

He was still alive and the other man wasn't, and there was no shame in that.

"Unhand me!"

A common refrain on a battlefield, but the voice that rang out in the still night was much too unusual to go unheeded: an angry, feminine vibrato.

Elijah poked his head up, scanning his surroundings. Night had fallen and thick cloud cover obscured the stars, making it hard to see much of anything. He squinted, wondering if he was simply going mad from fear until he saw the ethereal form burst through the mist-laced trees a few feet away from him. She was tall, perhaps as tall as him, and clad in a long, ivory gown that flowed around her feet as she ran. A hooded cloak obscured her features. When she stopped and turned, the cloak flapped in the wind, revealing a glint of metal clutched in her hand.

A stocky man with a rifle slung over his shoulder stumbled out of the woods close behind her, out of breath from giving chase. The man's impeccably tailored red coat, fine stockings, and imperious gait advertised that he was a high-ranking officer in His Majesty's Army.

"You've caused quite enough trouble tonight, Kate," the man said between huffs. "You'll return to my tent this instant, before we end up in the thick of the battle."

A squabble with a camp follower, Elijah thought with contempt. He must have run further than he'd thought. He would hunker down until these two took their drama elsewhere, and then attempt to find his way back to his fellow Continentals.

"I'll be damned if I do that," the woman bit out in a familiarly accented voice. It had the dips and curves of the voices of the older women in the slave quarters, those who had not been born with a shackle linking them to these fledgling colonies.

A gust of cold wind whipped across the marsh, knocking the woman's hood back, and Elijah felt a tremor run through him that was entirely unrelated to the weather. Her kinky hair was cut short, exposing smooth dark skin pulled taut across high cheekbones and a proud forehead. Her eyes were narrowed and her full lips stretched into a grimace as she regarded the Redcoat who approached her. She was gorgeous in her fury.

Kate, Elijah thought, feeling a strange throb of anger at the dull British name likely bestowed upon her by her owners, just as his had been. It in no way matched the woman before him.

"I was told that if I fled my rebel master and joined with the Crown I'd have my freedom," she said. "There was no mention of bartering my body for the privilege. I will work, but not on my back. If you think I traveled this far just to be ravished by some bloody English bastard, you are quite mistaken."

"Come now, girl," the man crooned, his voice placating. "Don't act as if you're stranger to a good tupping. I said I'd give you a bit of coin, what more do you want?"

"So romantic, you Brits," she sneered. "Is that how your father wooed your mother before he rutted with her, then?"

"You disrespectful bitch. I'll—" the man grabbed for her. Elijah didn't know if the Redcoat saw the flash of the knife but he surely felt its point as the woman drove it into his sternum. The Englishman's face went white with shock and he clasped the knife with both hands, tumbling to his knees before he could pull it free. The woman called Kate stood over him and watched, her face expressionless.

She didn't even flinch, Elijah thought. As if she'd heard him, she suddenly began to shake. It was cold, but not enough to cause the full body tremors that wracked the woman as she pulled her cloak close and stared at the dead man at her feet.

Elijah knew he should stay where he was and wait for this morbid tableau to come to its logical conclusion, with the woman fleeing into the night.

Bloody hell, he thought as he pulled himself from the ditch and started for her. His mother had always told him that his heart was bigger than his brain.

He stepped on a branch as he approached, and the noise startled her. The clouds had passed and wan moonlight illuminated her gaze as she turned to face him. Her eyes were filled with a fear that made his heart constrict. It made no sense, given the harsh words and deadly action he'd just witnessed, but in that moment she seemed like something fragile that should be held gently. A newly bloomed rose whose delicate petals might fall away at the slightest touch, despite her sharp thorns.

"Are you alright?" He walked toward her with hands raised. Dealing with skittish animals was his job, and the woman before him was not so different from a wild mare — one wrong move and she would bolt. He had to proceed with caution, lest he alarm her.

Her gaze flitted over his body, which he knew was a weapon in itself. A lifetime of plowing and planting and picking had seen to that.

She took a step back.

"I mean you no harm," he said. "I saw what the bastard was attempting and he deserved what he got."

She was still trembling, although her dark gaze had sharpened to better scrutinize him. Her face was so expressive that Elijah knew the instant she let a bit of her guard down. A bit was a lot for a woman like her, though. He was sure of that.

"Most of them aren't like that," she said. She pulled at her gown—up close, he could see how dirt clung to the tattered hem, how the fabric was worn from too many washings. "Most of the soldiers ignore me, unless they need me to launder or mend their uniforms. It was such a relief, after…after everything else. But this one, he fixed his attentions on me and he wouldn't look away. I couldn't let it happen again. It will *not* happen again."

There was something entrancing in the warm tones of her voice. It was quiet now, nearly carried away by the winds chasing the clouds through the night sky, but there was no mistaking the strength that undergirded her words.

Elijah walked over to the fallen man and began searching him. He'd gotten barely anything from the Regular in the ditch, but this man had a fine musket and an even finer revolver, plus a small satchel of coins. He took the weapons and tossed the coin purse to Kate. Her eyes widened in surprise as she clutched it, but she didn't seem pleased. It was only in that moment that Elijah realized he *wanted* to please her.

"I'm going to find my regiment now, if you want to come with me," he said. "The Loyalists scattered us, but I'm sure we're regrouping somewhere."

"You're fighting with the Continentals?" she asked. Elijah felt an uncharacteristic surge of pride, but that was quickly crushed under the weight of her next words. "Are you daft?"

Surprise froze him first, and then Elijah's temper flared. Suddenly, he was acutely regretting coming to Kate's aid. He hadn't been wrong in his initial assessment: she was a hard woman.

"Is it daft to fight for my country?" he asked. "This is my homeland, and I mean to defend it."

He believed those words, believed them with all his soul, despite the way things were now. Things could be different after the Colonies were free of the taxes meted out by the British, different for him and everyone else trapped by the bonds of slavery. That he had other motivations for fighting, a deal struck between master and slave, was none of her concern.

"You speak like a man with book learning. A freedman, perhaps?" she guessed, her hand gripping the coin purse. "I bet you grew up in some Northern town and have white neighbors who treat you nice. Well, let me remind you: you are a nigger and your country enslaves niggers. Yet you risk your life to help these men. Yes, I'd call that quite daft."

Elijah's anger was sudden and intense. She thought she knew what he had been through, did she? Maybe he would strip his shirt off and show her how wrong she was.

"Oh, so the British are our great saviors, are they?" he asked, annoyed by her icy disapproval and his reaction to it. "Says the woman who just killed one of the bastards for trying to molest her. Perhaps you'd like to ask our brethren down in the islands their opinion?"

It was only after her warm wrist was in his grip that Elijah realized he was touching her and, worse, that his actions mirrored those of the British officer. Kate's knife was still lodged in her attacker's chest, so she didn't stab Elijah. She simply stared back at him with a disdain that was as cutting as any blade.

She whipped her arm around before he could release her, the quick movement freeing her from his grip and placing space between them. Her aim with the knife hadn't been lucky; she knew how to fight.

"Don't mistake my choice for approval. The British are simply the lesser of two evils," Kate said flatly. "Some folk may choose to stick with the devil they know. But the devil you know is still a devil, and when this war is over, he'll send you straight to hell whether he wins or loses."

Her words stung. It wasn't as if he hadn't had the same thoughts himself. It would be foolish not to consider every option, especially with the Crown offering freedom to those slaves who deserted their Patriot masters and joined with them. But fighting for the Colonists provided Elijah an opportunity for freedom, too, and he wouldn't have to leave his homeland to get it.

"The Crown makes a tidy sum selling the likes of us, in addition to taxing the Colonists for breathing," Elijah retorted. "Yet I suppose you imagine they'll set you up with a house along the Thames when this ends. Now who's daft?"

They stared at each other, and Elijah fought the urge to look away from the conviction in her gaze. He'd made the right decision—of that he was sure—but the way Kate looked at him as if he were a natural-born fool gave him the slightest pause, and one that wasn't entirely ideological.

He shouldn't have found her beautiful. She was rude, abrasive, and had insulted his intelligence. But his gaze was already fastened on her luscious mouth when it pulled up into a mirthless smile.

"Many thanks for your offer of assistance, but, having tried slavery once, I find it's not to my liking. I'll be returning to the British camp, where at least I'm paid to be held in contempt," she said.

"And I'll be returning to my regiment, where I'll fight for freedom for everyone, including those who turn their backs on their homeland," Elijah retorted, and then wished he hadn't. The words sounded naive even to him. Kate's assessing gaze goaded something in him, though, something that had him shivering in a marsh and hoping she'd warm him with her heated words instead of leaving him to find his compatriots.

"This is not my homeland," she said, her accent reinforcing her words. "But I wish you well in your endeavor…"

"Elijah," he supplied. He didn't know what compelled him. He would never see her again, but some part of him was adamant that she know him, if only in this small way. "Elijah Sutton."

She nodded and stuffed the coin purse into a pocket in the lining of her cloak.

"Good evening to you, Elijah."

She turned back in the direction she'd come from, just as a group of Redcoats emerged from the woods. Everything went still as the four soldiers took in the scene: Kate, who sparked recognition in their eyes; Elijah, who wore the uniform of the enemy; and the crumpled form of one of their officers on the ground. In a flash, three of the men were on him, wrestling him to the ground while the other turned over the body.

"It's Trumbull! He's killed Trumbull!"

Elijah grunted in protest as they pulled the dead man's weapon from his back. His eyes flashed to Kate. All signs of the woman who gave cheek at every opportunity and could kill a man with one blow were gone. Her head was bowed demurely as she murmured, "It all happened so fast."

"Why is the washwoman here?" one of the men holding him down asked.

"Good question," Elijah said, and received a cuff to the ear for his trouble.

Kate's eyes widened, gaze flying frantically from soldier to soldier.

"He—, I—," she stammered, and then without the slightest warning she fell into a dead faint.

"Bloody hell," one of the soldiers said. "Tie this one up. We'll put him with the other prisoners. One of you boys pick her up. We'll have to send some boys back for the body."

As the men trussed him like game fowl, Elijah glared at Kate's prone form. One eye fluttered open and then quickly squeezed shut when she saw him staring at her.

He growled in frustration. His mother had been right. Large heart, small brain, indeed.

CHAPTER 2

KATE IGNORED the fact that the young soldier carrying her occasionally allowed himself a surreptitious caress of her bottom as he hauled her back to the encampment. A stolen squeeze through her gown was better than him shaking her awake and demanding answers. And she'd endured far worse in her life. Far worse.

She wanted to attempt another peek at her surroundings, but the last time she'd chanced it, Elijah had been staring at her with a fury that made her want to faint in truth. She regretted his capture, but he was the enemy and would have been treated as such regardless of whether he'd stopped to make sure she was alright. Her admitting to killing Trumbull wouldn't help either of them.

Well, maybe it would help him a bit, she admitted, but there was no benefit in thoughts like that. She'd promised herself she would survive at any cost, and the life of a handsome stranger was a price she was willing to pay.

Yes, he was handsome, undeniably so. He was a large man, larger than any man at the British camp, that was certain. He had frightened her half to death when he loomed up out of the night like a haint from a scary tale.

When he'd gotten closer, though, she'd been taken aback for another reason entirely. His fine face with its strong jaw and wide, sinful mouth had thrilled her, even as she shook in the aftermath of Trumbull's demise. And his eyes…the women in the slave quarters called eyes like Elijah's "bedchamber eyes" because they made you think of what a man could do to you if he got you alone near a pallet. Elijah Sutton hadn't even been trying, and he'd had her stomach in knots and her heart pounding. Maybe that was why she'd been so unforgivably rude to him in spite of the fact that he'd come to her aid.

Kate didn't trust kindness from strangers; people always wanted something in return, and often more than she was willing to pay. Trusting a stranger had landed her in shackles on a cramped and filthy boat, stripped from a family that she could barely remember now. She couldn't even recall her true name. She'd forgotten it long ago, left it behind on the Carolina auctioneer's block where she'd been dubbed Kate. America had stolen even that from her, and yet Elijah would have her consider this country her home?

"Take him to the stables," one of the soldiers said. "Put him with the others we captured tonight."

The soldier carrying her unceremoniously dropped her onto the ground, heaving from the exertion.

"I thought Negresses were supposed to be made of hardier stuff than this," he huffed, poking at her with the tip of his boot.

Kate began to stir, facing the unfortunate fact that she couldn't simply lie prone forever.

"What happened?" she asked. She was sure to keep her voice faint and high, and to blink up at the soldiers like the calves she used to shoulder aside to do the milking.

"Where is Trumbull? He asked me to help him carry something, and then, and then…"

She cocked her head to the side, as if waiting for them to complete the sentence. She'd seen her mistress play the role of dainty, overly taxed woman often enough. Of course, she didn't have the porcelain complexion to reinforce it, but perhaps she could still pull it off.

The soldiers regarded her for a long moment.

"You don't remember?" her human pack mule asked. His tone implied he was rather unconvinced.

"Remember what?" she asked. Another flurry of blinks. "Has something happened?"

"Trumbull is dead. You and the big black bloke were the only ones there when we arrived."

"I don't remember anything," Kate said. She didn't have to fake the tremble in her voice. If they discovered she'd killed Trumbull, it wouldn't matter that it had been in defense of her virtue; to them she possessed no such thing. She'd hang. "I don't know what man you speak of. I came to this camp alone, and I remain so. All I know for certain is that my head aches terribly."

The soldier squinted down at her for a long moment.

"Well, the Captain'll be wanting to speak with you." the soldier said. "Go back to your people for now."

I have no people, she thought reflexively, and that knowledge almost made her sink back to the ground. She rose unsteadily to her feet and slowly navigated her way to the Black encampment, barely noticing as the orderly rows of canvas tents grew shabbier and the path more littered with debris.

Here, instead of orders being shouted at Regulars, mothers called for their children to come eat their dinner. Instead of drifting in from the skirmish, the men were returning from constructing battlements, blacksmithing, and the countless other types of hard labor the Negroes who had enlisted with the Loyalists performed. Very few of them had been armed and sent into battle, as they'd imagined when they sided with the British. It was leaps and bounds better than the life most people had escaped, though, so complaints were saved for hushed tones around camp fires and the modest privacy of the tents.

Kate's thoughts drifted to Elijah, to his pride in fighting for a country that seemed to hate people who looked like them. How could it be otherwise? Her master often told his slaves he loved them. He told them as they toiled in the field, and when he lashed them "for their own good." And that's what he'd told her when he pulled her out of the slave quarters in the middle of the night and lifted her tattered skirts...everything Kate knew of "love" made her wish to never hear the word again. Still...

What would it be like to be loved by a man like Elijah Sutton? A man who was strong and kind-hearted? some foolish part of her wondered. Perhaps Elijah was different from the others who'd taken and taken until there was nothing left of her but a hard heart and a desire to live driven by vitriol alone.

Perhaps. And perhaps such fantasies are what cost you everything once before.

A small form rocketed toward Kate, pulling her from her confusing thoughts. She opened her arms and caught up the laughing toddler who pounced on her, settling the small but solid girl on her hip.

"Charlotte, it's too late for you to be out by yourself. Where is your mama?" she asked as she hugged the girl to her. Oh, that warmth was familiar, as was the sour sweet smell that meant the girl was due for a scrubbing. Kate's chest burned with the memory of another child she had once bundled in her arms.

Charlotte's mother had managed to keep her daughter safe after escaping from a Maryland plantation and searching out British troops. Kate couldn't begrudge Lettie that, but she would always envy her.

Well, she didn't have a bastard of a husband to lead her astray, did she? Kate thought bitterly. *She wasn't a foolish chit who thought a man asking before he laid with you meant he cared enough to protect you.*

"She's a slippery little thing!" Lettie said as she ducked through the flap of their tent and stepped out into the cool night air. She reached for her daughter, and Kate handed the girl over with a pang. She pushed the feeling away, steeled herself against too much fondness for the child. Allowing such an attachment to shatter her world again could not be allowed.

"Are you well?" Lettie asked, ignoring her daughter's babbling and turning a serious gaze toward Kate. "Word came down from the camp that Trumbull had got himself killed, and last I saw him, he was pulling you off into the dark."

Kate's blood ran cold. She and Lettie were friendly, but she trusted no one. The urge to run, familiar as her own heartbeat in the still of the night, welled up in her.

"I won't tell anyone what I saw!" Lettie said, reaching out to pat Kate's arm. Kate thought of Trumbull's grip on her earlier, and then of Elijah's. She pressed her lips together and Lettie smiled uncertainly and moved her hand away. "I just wanted to be sure you were unharmed. You always look after Charlotte when I need to rest, and you've been so kind to us. I'd hate it if any harm had come to you."

Kate let out a deep breath.

"I am well," she assured Lettie, but her head was beginning to swim, despite her reassurance. The events of the night were catching up with her, and she suddenly felt a fatigue that emanated from someplace deep within, one she was uncertain that even sleep would offer reprieve from. She wanted food and her bedroll, and to be free of thoughts of Trumbull and Elijah and children she'd never hug again.

"Then I am glad," Lettie said with relief. "Do you want to join us for a meal?"

"Many thanks, but I'm exhausted."

Hoofbeats approached and a young Regular pulled his horse up beside them. Charlotte reached her hand toward the creature with a squeal of delight and Lettie turned to keep her a safe distance from the panting horse.

"You're needed to assist with tending to the prisoners being held at the Pieterse farm," he said with unwarranted impatience. "Leave the babe and come along."

"Are we not allowed rest? We've both worked all day and into the night," Kate said, hoping to sway him.

"And you'll work a bit more," he replied. "I was told to stop the first colored women I came upon and bring them to aid the soldiers."

"I'll ask one of the others to take care of Charlotte," Lettie said. Her tired gaze rested regretfully on the daughter she had spent the entire day away from.

"No. You must rest, Lettie. Charlotte is enough to handle on top of the work you've done all day," Kate said, and then turned to the soldier. "I'll go."

"Both of you are needed," he said, obviously attempting to follow the order he had been given.

"I can do the work of two," Kate said and started off, away from Lettie, before the man could contradict her.

"Very well." His horse trotted past her, toward the farm, kicking dirt up into her face as he went.

She spent the walk to the farm bracing herself against the fact that Elijah would likely be amongst the prisoners. He had grabbed her during their first encounter, although he hadn't wanted to hurt her. Kate had learned to detect that inclination in a man, which is why she had lodged her knife into Trumbull with no regrets. But being taken prisoner could raise a man's ire, so she'd have to be on her guard.

If he hasn't already been blamed for Trumbull's murder and killed. She didn't like thinking of his hope, however misplaced, being extinguished.

The perimeter of the barn was chaotic: soldiers patrolling, wounded men being treated or begging for aide, guns and the other spoils of war stripped from the prisoners being sorted.

Kate was handed a bucket of water with a ladle and shoved toward the barn door, where the clamor and stench nearly pushed her back outside. The structure was large, but not large enough for the dozens of men packed inside. There were Patriots in ragged uniforms covering every surface. Many of them were injured, and Kate's gaze shied away from those bloody, hopeless men as she ladled water for the thirsty prisoners to drink.

She was on her fourth bucket and starting to feel something strangely like worry when she finally saw him. She heard the familiar timbre of his voice emanating from a corner of the barn, where he sat beside a man who lay stretched out on the ground. She wondered at the wide berth being given to them, but then she saw the way the man shook as Elijah took off his coat and tucked it around his prone form. Soldiers avoided death at all cost, even in close quarters. The reaper had surely come for this man, but Elijah was beside him all the same.

"And then General Washington walked by, and you could sense the gaze of every man stuck fast to him — not a one of us could look away," Elijah said in a tone that was much too jovial, given their predicament. He laughed, and then held his arm out in front of the man's face. "You could feel his presence in the very air, raising the hairs on the backs of your wrists. It was marvelous! Ever hear of the divine right of kings? How a king is chosen by God to rule over his people? I didn't believe in it until that very moment. If anyone can lead our country to freedom, rest assured it is him."

All Kate knew of Washington was that he owned slaves and that he didn't wanted colored men to fight for the Patriots, but damned if Elijah's vivid words didn't raise gooseflesh on her sore arms.

"I never got to see him with my own eyes, and now I shan't," the man said in a reedy New England accent. "I'm going to die, you know."

"Perhaps. We all do eventually. Not everyone gets to do it fighting for a worthy cause." For a moment his gaze was hard and focused elsewhere, but then he stared down at the man. "If you do, it won't be in vain," he vowed. His head turned and she saw the instant when he realized she was standing there. She waited for him to yell, to jump up and shake her, to demand she clear his name. Instead, he smiled.

"Are you thirsty, Michael? There's a beautiful woman waiting to water you, so I think you should say yes."

"Yes," Michael echoed weakly. Elijah moved to sit cross-legged and then gently lifted the man's sweat-soaked head and placed it into his lap. Now that Kate could see his face, she realized Michael was young, barely in his fifteenth year if she guessed correctly. His cheeks were still round where time would have made them lean and hard, and his cherubic face was deathly pale where tears had streaked through the layer of dirt and gore.

Elijah gave her an imploring look, and Kate understood what he wanted of her. She took a few steps closer and then knelt beside them.

"Good evening to you, Michael," she said in a voice so full of cheer she hardly recognized it as her own. "Did you know the other Patriots here are using horse muck for pillows? You have the most comfortable seat in this entire barn."

The boy chuckled and then coughed, the sound thick and horrible.

"That wouldn't be the first time a woman has proclaimed my lap to be a most comfortable resting place," Elijah said loftily.

Kate paused as she dipped the ladle into the cool water, heat rushing to her cheeks at his bawdy words. She was suddenly disconcerted, unsure of Elijah's intent. Then she heard Michael laugh again and took the words for what they were: something to ease a dying boy's pain.

She shot Elijah a warning glance, and then brought the ladle to Michael's lips. Even with Elijah steadying his head, most of the water ended up spilling down the boy's cheeks. Still, after three ladles he leaned back with a content smile on his face.

"Thank you," he said, his voice softer now, so that Kate had to lean in close to hear him. Elijah did, too, so that their foreheads nearly touched. "Tell mother I love her, will you? And Diane McGregor, too."

With that, his eyes fluttered shut and did not open. His trembling stilled beneath Elijah's jacket, and his face settled into an expression that was too serene to be confused with slumber.

Kate dropped the ladle into the bucket and swiped at the moisture leaking from her eyes. Why was she crying for this soldier boy who she didn't know from Adam? One who fought for a country that held her in bondage and called itself a harbinger of freedom? She'd thought herself done with such foolish displays of emotion, but her throat burned with a suppressed sob that said otherwise.

"This is the second time we've met with a body between us," Elijah said as he slid from beneath Michael, gently placing the boy's head on the ground. "I'd hope for it to be the last, but with this bloody war on that seems rather unlikely."

Kate glanced at Elijah's face, at the way his lips were drawn into a grim smile that didn't match the grief in his eyes.

"I'm sorry," she said, grateful that her voice didn't break. "Did you know him well?"

Elijah shook his head.

"Only as long as I've been held prisoner here. Our acquaintance was limited by the chest wound, you see."

Kate grabbed the pail and stood, unnerved by his answer. He had shown that level of kindness to a stranger? She wasn't used to men who behaved this way. Integrity had only been a word in her master's dictionary or a sermon from the visiting pastor.

He's in this place because he showed kindness to you, her conscience reminded her.

"Are you thirsty, Elijah?" she asked. She couldn't protect him from the wrath of the British or his own foolish hope, but she could offer him this small gesture.

He turned his deep brown eyes up to her — still striking, though they were now limned with exhaustion and sadness — and gave a brief nod. Her hand shook as she raised the ladle to his mouth, and water splattered on the dusty ground. She cursed her lack of control over her body, something she thought she had mastered, but Elijah cupped two warm hands around her trembling one and drank deeply.

He kept his eyes open as he quenched his thirst, his gaze locked on Kate's even after he'd had his fill. She couldn't help but stare back at him, wondering how the stubbled angles of his jaw and the moist curves of his lips would feel beneath her fingertips. She was abuzz with an odd sensation, as if she'd swallowed a wasp's nest.

"Thank you, Kate," he said. No more bawdy words, and no judgment or anger either.

"You're not like other men," she blurted out, ashamed as what was supposed to be a private thought tumbled from her lips.

"How so?" he asked, the intensity of his gaze making her feel even more exposed than her slip-up had.

"You're…" *Better*, she thought. "…different."

Elijah smiled. "Something tells me that, coming from you, this is a compliment. Two compliments from the prickly Kate just might make getting blamed for your crime worthwhile. A third might kill me, though, so please be sure to insult my intelligence now, or at the very least my mother."

They looked at each other for a long moment, and Kate struggled to think of something terrible to say to him, but all she could think of was that he might be in trouble because of her actions. Worse, she found that she actually cared what would happen to him.

"Elijah—"

Her words caught in the back of her throat.

"I was jesting, Kate," he said. "You should go. I'm going to say a prayer for Michael's soul now. Perhaps you could pay me the same courtesy."

Kate nodded and stumbled away from him, away from the strange feelings he conjured in her that were at distinct odds with her resolve. Even though she had long ceased believing in a higher power, her thought as she turned away from him was *Heavenly father, I hope I haven't condemned this man.*

CHAPTER 3

ELIJAH COUNTED off three days since his capture. Redcoats had come to remove bodies from the barn that first morning after the battle, dragging them out to a mass grave, but all had been quiet since then. No one had questioned him about Trumbull's death; either it had been forgotten as the British worked to secure their hold on Brooklyn or they acknowledged the man wasn't worth a damn. There had been no discussion of what would be done with the prisoners. There had been no food or water, either.

Elijah's stomach cramped painfully as he lay on the floor, awakened by hunger pangs. He wished he could fall back to sleep—time passed slowly when every second was spent anticipating when your next meal would arrive. The warbling of the morning birds that eased the sun over the horizon with their song confused him—sunlight usually followed the bird song, but darkness still reigned beyond the cracks in the wooden slats of the barn.

Elijah scanned the space, taking in the huddled silhouettes of his fellow prisoners. He had thought the Continental Army sad when compared to the finery and might of the Crown's fighting forces, but now they were wretched by any standards. The last thing Elijah had eaten was a wizened apple he'd found beneath a tuft of hay. Now even the hay was gone, chewed by starving prisoners in search of the slightest bit of nourishment. The air of the barn was befouled by the odor of unwashed bodies and of the stall that had become a makeshift latrine. Even horses were allowed the dignity of a stable boy to shovel their muck.

He sighed and thought of the farm outside of the city, the place he had called home for so many years. He missed the peaceful feeling of being astride one of the horses he cared for, controlling a powerful creature that he had brought to heel with hours of hard work. Some men thought one must use force to gain control over an animal, that the will of another being was something to be broken. Elijah knew that it simply took patience and self-control. If you couldn't control a beast without resorting to force, it was a sign of your weakness, not your strength. Men from miles around, and even out of state, brought their animals to him, filling his master's coffers. It was hard, backbreaking work, but the excitement of getting a strong-willed creature to give itself up to his control — because it wanted to — was incomparable.

An image of Kate flashed in Elijah's mind then and he tried, unsuccessfully, to push it away; this exercise had become a regular occurrence during his imprisonment. He endeavored to hate her, to drive her from his thoughts, but what had she really done? She hadn't invited him to address her out on the marsh and place himself in the path of roving lobsterbacks. If he had kept to his own affairs, he would have made his way back to his regiment and never thought of her again. But since he hadn't, he'd been able to see her kindness as she watered the prisoners, circling the barn several times to make sure no man had been overlooked. He'd seen her sympathy for a dying stranger. He'd seen the flash of something hot in her eyes and the shaking of her hand beneath his, as if she were a shy girl instead of a woman able to kill in her own defense. Elijah's grief and fear and mortality had gotten all jumbled up in him in those moments after Michael's death, and he'd wanted nothing more than to pull Kate flush against him and let her warmth remind him that he was alive.

He remembered the tears escaping the dark pools of her eyes and the way her hand had felt clasped between his: he'd touched her supple skin and soothed the tremor of tendons and fragile bones, and it left him wanting more.

He'd sent her away that night, but in his imagination she returned many times over. The unwashed captives vanished and they were alone in the barn. In the private space concocted by his mind, he pulled her close, tasted her lush lips, and ran his hands over the subtle curvature of her body. He shushed her cutting remarks by lashing her with his tongue until she begged him for release. He plunged into her and they climaxed in a shuddering, sweaty act of mutual supplication. Hell, if impure thoughts of Kate were sustenance, Elijah would be round and gouty from his feasting.

But thoughts of a woman determined to turn her back on the Colonies had no place in his life. His future was in America. Elijah rolled onto his side on the hard floor of the barn, as if the strange pull he felt toward Kate was something he could turn his back on.

"Sutton, you awake?"

"Aye, Wallace, I am."

The wiry New Englander with thinning hair and bulging eyes had taken a liking to Elijah, as had several other prisoners. Elijah was fairly certain that his size, and not his sparkling personality, was the key attractant, as escape was on every man's mind.

"Do you think we should try today?" Wallace whispered. "If General Washington could have spared the troops to burst in and free us, they would have done so already. We must fight now, for soon we'll be too weak."

Most of the men were already too weak, in truth, but Elijah simply grunted in response. They had been hoping to ambush the next group of soldiers that came in to feed them, but they had waited in vain. It would likely be suicide, but more than one soldier had already gone mad, banging on the doors of the crowded barn until his hands bled, pleading to be released all the while. They had been packed together since joining the Continental Army, but tight quarters were quite different when you chose them and when your enemy chose them for you.

Outside of the barn, the morning bustle of soldiers stirring sounded. Elijah tried to focus on only the most important challenge he faced, escaping from this place and returning to his regiment, but when the smell of breakfast wafted in he thought he might sell his very soul for a strip of pork fat. He hadn't cried since he'd been pulled from his mother's arms as a gangly youth, but he came close as the delicious scents assaulted him.

"Bastards," he groaned as he clutched at his stomach. The door to the barn creaked open then, revealing a misty darkness caused by heavy fog. Several soldiers with loaded muskets marched in and trained their weapons on the prisoners. An imposing man decked out in a long uniform coat of the deepest scarlet and with an elaborate powdered wig stepped into the room behind them. Ornamentation at the lapels of his coat signaled his importance, as did the fine fabric of his uniform compared to the Regulars. His nostrils flared and he pulled a handkerchief, likely scented, from the sleeve of his coat and held it to his nose.

"I am Captain Nathaniel Bellamy and I'd have your attention, you pack of filthy reprobates," he bellowed. His voice was deep and resonant, and any man who had been asleep when he walked in was surely awake now.

"I'm no expert on the psyche of the American Colonist," he began when he knew he had their attention. He was obviously a man who enjoyed an audience. "The seditious acts committed by you and your so-called commanders have given me cause to travel to these shores for the first time, and, on the whole, I find you miserable and ignorant. Hypocrites of the highest order, crying for freedom while owning human chattel, and entirely crude, although I do admit that there is some charm to your thinking you can win against the Crown.

"However, given the length of my military service, I do know about soldiers in general and about those who have been taken prisoner in particular. You spend your free time plotting your escape, and when not engaged in that futile endeavor, imagining that the cavalry will soon arrive to free you. I have come to tell you that neither of those things will pass under my watch."

Elijah raised himself to a sitting position and glared at the man. The tension in the room was palpable; Bellamy's drawn-out theatrics were shredding the already fragile nerves of every prisoner.

"Say what you mean to say and be done with it," Elijah said, his voice raspy with fatigue and irritation. Every head, and a few musket barrels, turned in his direction, and there were rumbles of approval from the prisoners. The soldiers remained silent as they waited for a cue from Bellamy.

Elijah expected a reprimand, but Bellamy simply stared at him for a long moment before continuing.

"Very well. This morning, it was discovered that Mr. Washington and his army had fled during the night, using heavy fog to hide his cowardly evasion. Brooklyn has been reclaimed by the Crown and the island of Manhattan will surely follow."

He said the words with relish, emphasizing his insult to Washington's rank. He momentarily lowered his handkerchief and revealed the smile he sported as he took in their dismay.

Elijah's empty stomach lurched at the words, and the groans and gasps of his fellow Patriots rose around him.

It couldn't be. General Washington had taken flight? They'd known the city would be hard to hold without a naval fleet, that the Americans were vastly outnumbered, but this was a devastating blow. Elijah thought of Kate's words about the devil you know. Maybe she hadn't been mistaken.

Where tension had recently filled the barn to the rafters, despair now crept in.

"Most of you will be moved to the prison ships docked at Gravesend," Bellamy said, hands clasped behind his back and gaze searching the faces of the broken-spirited Patriots. "Some of you will remain to be used as labor. And some of you will need to answer an important question."

There was a bustle from behind Bellamy. In the breaks in the fog, Elijah could make out swaying skirts and dark skin. His eyes searched for that familiar straight-backed stance, but his vision was obstructed by the blanket of mist. The Captain continued.

"You few Colored soldiers: stand and come with me."

Elijah's eyes flew to the lean, ochre-skinned man seated a few yards away from him. A million speculations flew in the gaze they shared.

Is this related to Trumbull's death? Elijah wondered, hesitating. Perhaps he had been mistaken to assume that the ramifications of the battle would overshadow the loss of one vile Englishman. He should speak up, before each man with dark skin was punished in his stead.

"Come along." Bellamy snapped his fingers and a few of his men stepped into the barn, pulling out the handful of visibly Negro soldiers and forcing them toward the door.

They shuffled out, slowed by their dwindling energy reserves. For just a moment Elijah thought of slipping away as the Captain walked ahead of them, head held high, but then two of the armed soldiers detached and followed behind them.

"Kate, Lettie, bring breakfast for these men," the Captain said as he passed the group of colored women that had assembled near the barn. Elijah heard the rustle of skirts, and then there she was beside him. He tried to catch Kate's eye but she turned away as soon as he glanced at her, as if she had already been watching him. She quickly became a silhouette in the fog; it swallowed her up as if she had never been there. When she disappeared from his sight, Elijah felt something within him strain after her.

It's your belly, he thought ruefully. *You're so starved, you're willing to resort to cannibalism right now.* But as he trudged forward with the other men, it was feasting of another sort that hovered at the edges of his thoughts. He was surprised to learn that a starving man could desire more than food, although he reassured himself that this ridiculous fixation would dissipate as soon as he had eaten and his brain was fully functional.

A large white tent loomed up before them.

"You may wash here," the captain said, directing them to a barrel of water a few feet away from the tent's entrance. It was an order, not a kindness.

The men stripped their shirts and waistcoats and scrubbed, passing a lump of soap between them. The cool water was invigorating, and it felt damned good to scrub away the grime of the last few days. They were presented with clean shirts, of much finer quality than the tattered ones they had just shed. Elijah's was too small, and he heard feminine giggles as he struggled into it. He turned, hoping to hear Kate's laughter, but she stood staring at his back with a haunted look on her face. She had seen the scars, then.

After receiving a slightly better fitting shirt, he turned and entered the candlelit space of the tent, and the other men followed him. The captain was seated at the head of a large, roughly hewn wooden table, likely looted from one of the homes nearby. He waved his hand to indicate that the prisoners should take their places in the other seats.

The tent flap opened again and the women entered, carrying pots of tea and plates laden with buttered bread and roast meat. Elijah's stomach cramped tightly at the bevy of scents and he crossed his arms over his chest to restrain himself. His thoughts warred against each other, pride struggling valiantly against hunger. A dark hand with long, tapered fingers placed a plate down in front of him. He looked up to find Kate gazing at him, one brow slightly lifted in annoyance. Elijah wondered if his sudden dizziness was a result of his close proximity to the woman or to the food she held.

"A starved man can neither turn coat nor fight back," Kate whispered as she poured his tea. Was he that easy to read, or was she chiding all of the soldiers? He watched her make her rounds: unless she was an accomplished ventriloquist, he was the only man to receive her admonition. He picked up his bread and ate, relief swelling him down to the cell as he chewed and swallowed.

Bellamy watched as they ate, and Kate stood against the wall behind the man, ready to serve if so asked. She stared into the distance, avoiding Elijah's curious gaze.

"Now, I will be plain with you men: the Crown offers Negroes freedom and the Continentals do not."

The man beside Elijah choked on his bread, and Elijah gave him a hearty pound on the back. Bellamy sipped his tea as if he hadn't just nudged them toward treason, and then came right out with it.

"If you side with the Crown, you will be granted freedom when your service is complete, be it here, England, or one of our other colonies. It is as simple as that. Has your Mr. Washington made such an offer, or has he been too busy counting his losses?"

Elijah looked around the room, at the Black women bustling to serve and clear. Was this the brave new world that the British were offering? If so, it looked very similar to the one they were being offered relief from.

The other Patriots considered their food, chewing slowly to give themselves more time in which to respond. Elijah wiped at his mouth with a napkin, and placed it on the table beside his empty plate.

"I've seen nary a black face in your ranks, sir," Elijah said. "I've seen these women used as serving wenches, much as they are at my master's estate. Why should I trust anything you have to say?"

The Captain's smirk faltered, but only for a second. Behind him, Kate stared at Elijah with wide eyes. He remembered that she had thought him a freedman, and apparently the whip lashes crisscrossing his back hadn't fully disabused her of that notion.

"You don't have to trust me, just as I don't *have* to offer you and your compatriots' freedom. I do so because a man I admire greatly, Lord Dunmore, believes it is the right course of action. You might be especially valuable to me because you have some experience soldiering and a natural tendency toward leadership, if I interpret your insouciance kindly." He looked at Elijah with a possessive gleam in his eyes, one not very different from the men who had squeezed his muscles and stuck their fingers in his mouth when he was sold off. "You could train Negro regiments, and lead them in battle. But if you wish to see how our colored forces are treated in the meantime, I will allow one of them to show you. Kate—"

He raised his hand without looking behind him, as if knowing that she would come when he beckoned. An unfamiliar sensation swept over Elijah: jealousy. When Kate stepped up next to the Captain, head bowed subserviently, Elijah wanted to shake her. Where was the strong woman who managed to rile him every time he encountered her? Why should this Captain choose her out of all the women? What did she mean to him?

"Since you seem to have elected yourself as the representative of this group, Kate will show you around the Negro encampment. You can report your findings back to them upon your return."

"You're allowing me to travel through these camps alone with a woman as my guide?" Elijah asked, hoping his surprise covered his irrational annoyance. What designs the Captain had on Kate was the least of his problems, or should have been.

"I trust you to return, as I'm sure you don't want these men to pay for your escape attempt with their lives," the Captain said easily. "Besides, Kate hates the Colonies as much as we do. I have complete faith in her ability to change your mind."

Elijah had to concede that the Captain was canny. He had already isolated the colored soldiers from the rest of the prisoners by giving them special treatment. When word got back to the barn, they would likely be treated with suspicion. Now, he was singling Elijah out and sending him off with a beautiful woman, sure to raise the ire of the handful of troops who'd been pulled out with him. Envy was a useful tool for those who knew how to wield it.

Elijah stood, looking at Kate and not the Captain when he spoke.

"You may show me your camp, and I shall report back to these men." He then turned to his fellow prisoners. "I will not be moved, but I will speak truthfully when I give my accounting."

It took more than a pretty face to change his allegiance, but if this was to be his only chance to get a lay of the land and plan an escape, it wouldn't hurt to have Kate at his side while he plotted.

CHAPTER 4

KATE WAS positive Elijah could hear her heart hammering in her chest as they walked through the dissipating mist. The day was warming, but she was sure the heat that enveloped her body was entirely a result of Elijah's presence.

For three days, she had worried about how he fared. She'd loitered near the barn in her off hours, telling herself she was needed in the area but really waiting on the chance that something, anything, would happen with the prisoners.

She hadn't been able to stop thinking of how gently his callused hands had cupped hers, of how his dark gaze had penetrated her as he drank from her ladle. Kate had considered her carnal urges so many cold ashes in the wind, but in that moment some latent ember had flared and flamed high, and now the heat of it would not leave her.

This was madness. There was a war on, and they were on opposite sides of it. It didn't matter that she'd laid on the hard ground of her tent and imagined his weight on top of her. That his smile was branded in her mind, a constant reminder of everything she couldn't have.

He was not for her.

She explained the basic setup of the Negro encampment to Elijah as they walked: the tasks that were required of them and the fact that men in the encampment were called troops but neither wore the uniform of the Loyalists nor carried their arms. Not yet at least.

He wasn't impressed, and she felt rather silly explaining what sounded like just another form of impressment in the face of his skepticism. Still, life in the camp was a foundation for something better than the life America promised them. She knew that.

Perhaps he'll change his mind yet, she thought. *Perhaps you can make him change it.*

She brushed the dangerous thoughts away. Elijah Sutton was not her priority. Freedom was. She wasn't quite sure what she'd do once she reached England or Canada, but the only thing that mattered was getting away from this place that had taken everything from her.

She glanced up at Elijah, although she knew without looking that he was keeping pace beside her. She could sense the strength emanating from him. She couldn't help but wonder if there was some lucky woman who knew the shelter of his muscular arms and the power of his embrace. He looked like he knew how to hold a woman, how to make her forget...

"I know what you're thinking," he said abruptly. He had been staring straight ahead, but his gaze darted in her direction now.

Kate stopped and dropped her gaze to the sparse grass shoots struggling up through the well-trodden ground.

"Pardon?" she asked, her face growing even warmer.

"You're thinking that because Washington retreated, I'll feel betrayed and easily switch allegiance," he said, his eyes scanning the hustle and bustle around them. "You can drive such foolishness from your head right now. My constancy isn't dependent upon one man. There are other factors, and other people, to think of."

"Oh. Right," Kate sighed with relief that he hadn't somehow intuited her libidinous thoughts before realizing that his response was the opposite of what she wanted to hear.

"I'm intrigued," she said. "What could have such a hold on you here that you will not budge in your foolish loyalty?"

"Have you nothing that binds you to this land?" Elijah asked. Kate felt the delicate shell surrounding her private pain crack just a bit.

"No, I don't," she said. The tie that bound her had been lost by her own foolhardiness. Now nothing held her to this land, or this earth, except sheer spite. She realized that Elijah had stopped walking too and was plainly staring at her, his mouth drawn tight. She didn't like the pity in his eyes.

"You have a woman waiting at home for you to return from battle?" she asked, turning the focus back on him. "Let me guess, she's sweet as fresh milk and mild as a spring day."

Elijah snorted, following after her.

"There's a female waiting alright," he said, and Kate pretended she wasn't disappointed. "Name's Biscuit. She's about sixteen hands tall, seventy stone, and black as midnight."

Kate cut her gaze in his direction as he smiled at her, really smiled, the white of his teeth pressing into the dark berry of his plump lower lip. His eyes crinkled at the corners, his mirth heightening their sensuality instead of reducing it. His stubble had grown into a short beard, which suited him even better. He was beautiful, altogether, and Kate hadn't the slightest idea of how to react. She realized she was simply staring at him when one corner of his mouth dropped and he explained, "Biscuit is a horse, Kate."

Kate sucked her teeth and flounced ahead, her eyes on the working zone of the encampment ahead of them. "I understood that! I was simply appalled that you'd sell yourself so cheaply."

She knew she was being rude, but she couldn't seem to help it. Elijah was stirring feelings in her that she thought had been cauterized by the fire of painful reality. She had promised herself that she wouldn't care for anyone again, but the slightest attention from Elijah was making her question everything. Snapping at him was the only defense available to her, and it was certainly preferable to stabbing him.

He caught up to her, stepping into her path so that she was forced to look up at him. His mouth was tight again, but there was no pity in his eyes this time.

"I have an agreement with the man I've been calling master," Elijah said.

"The man who left those scars on your back?" she asked. She'd felt sick when she caught sight of the thick, raised flesh on his skin. Not from disgust, but from imagining a man as kind as Elijah whipped like an animal. From knowing that he'd endured that barbaric treatment and was still the type of man who'd stop to help a strange woman. Who'd speak against Bellamy just so his fellow soldiers thought that maybe they were brave enough to do the same.

"No," he said. "Master Sutton bought me several years back, and has been as kind to me as one can be to a man he owns like chattel," Elijah said tersely. "When this war arose, we struck up a deal: I'd fight in his stead, and if I returned I'd be given my freedom, some horses, and a parcel of land to conduct my business. That is why nothing you say or do will change my mind. I have a future here, you see, and I've earned every bit of it."

His intensity was entrancing. He wasn't yelling, and he didn't grab her as he did at their first meeting, but part of her wished he would. Then she could lash out again. Then he'd be like all the rest.

"And you believe him?" she asked.

"Yes," he said. "You believe that the British will pay your board to one of their holdings and settle you into a new life. Well, that sounds like a fantasy to me. My belief in Master Sutton, who I know to be a man of his word, is based solidly in reality, so I could do without you looking at me like I'm addled."

"You'll be free, but others will not," she said, searching for an argument that would ruffle him. Something about Elijah's steadfast belief in these Colonies made her want to fight him tooth and nail. "That's alright with you then?"

"Infuriating woman," he growled, taking a step closer. Even though he wasn't very much taller than her, that he was looking down at her in that moment was quite apparent.

"I said no such thing. When I'm free, I'll do what I can to free others. I know a group of men who work with that exact purpose in mind, and there are others like them. I wouldn't be able to effect much change from across the bloody Atlantic, would I? Although I suppose you've figured out some way to do it since you have the cheek to question me."

"I—" Kate had no retort for that. The truth was she had been worried about herself and her own pain for so many years that she had long since stopped caring about the plight of others. About individuals, yes, but freedom for the race as a whole had become an abstract. He'd caught her in a snare of her own words.

Impulsiveness had always been her downfall, and although losing an argument to a man she'd known for three days should hardly have been a world-shaking event, it was.

Have I chosen incorrectly, again? she thought in despair. For the briefest of moments she was back in the rushing river, fighting to keep a grip on the bundle in her arms.

It was only when Elijah's hand cupped her face and his thumb brushed over her cheek that she realized a shocked tear had fallen.

"It's all right, Katie," he said in a low voice that wrapped around her like a cool breeze. The way he murmured *Katie*...for the first time in memory she felt at ease with the name that had been chosen for her so carelessly, for Elijah spoke the appellation with such care. His hand moved up, sliding over her shorn hair and down her neck in a repetitive motion. "I'm sorry. No need for tears."

His touch felt wonderful. Too wonderful. It loosened something within her that needed to remain lodged solidly in place, the lodestone of her pain that kept her from crumbling.

She stepped away from him, ashamed at the sense of loss when she could no longer feel the heat of him against her. It was ridiculous: he was not hers, thus there was nothing to lose.

Kate cleared her throat and resumed the tour of the colored encampment. If there was one thing she knew well it was how to pretend that something hadn't occurred. She'd returned to her plantation all those years ago, sopping wet and arms empty, and acted as if her husband and child had never existed. Avoidance was old tack for her.

Elijah followed her lead, filling the silence with questions about their location and the movement of the British soldiers. He even asked about mundane things, like the washing schedules and when food was delivered; questions she answered dutifully, grateful for the distraction.

"If you have no plans to join the British, why did you agree to this?" she asked as they walked back along a path that cut through a dense section of forest.

"Because I have to report back to those men waiting in the Captain's tent. I don't presume to make their choice for them, even if I think they choose wrong."

Kate simply nodded. Hopefully, the men would be surer in their choice than she was. The Captain had dispatched her with the duty of recruiting Elijah Sutton, but the man had shaken her resolve. Worse, he had revealed her flaw to her and hadn't judged her for it. He'd treated her with kindness instead, and now she was lost.

"Are you willing to go to the prison ships for your patriotism? That's a veritable death sentence, although a noose would be kinder," she said. It was one last effort to change his mind and a reminder to herself where his decision would take him. If he didn't take Bellamy up on his offer, it wouldn't matter how he made her feel. Elijah would likely be a dead man.

She was asking a serious question, but he turned that glorious smile on her once more.

"If the lobsterbacks can get me onto that stinking ship, I'll gladly die for my country," he said. "But in case you haven't noticed, I'm not one to concede a point very easily, and death is a very final point."

She laughed, but then he took a step closer and her laughter died in her throat.

"But in case I'm not long for this world…"

He leaned in slowly, giving her time to escape. She did not run.

If the touch of his hand had moved her, the soft sweet press of his mouth shook her to her core. His lips were warm against hers, rubbing gently in a way that was both subdued and overwhelming. Kate had been kissed, for reasons ranging from passion to possession, but never as softly as this. Elijah's hands rested chastely on her arms, but the encircling warmth of them was a reminder of his strength — the strength he wasn't using against her. She could feel his ardor in the deepening of their kiss and the way his feet moved restlessly in the grass, but his hold on her was completely gentle.

"Elijah," she whispered because she was so full of emotion she had to say something and his name was her only release.

His barely suppressed groan vibrated against her lips, the sensation a precursor to the warmth of his tongue as he licked into her mouth. She mimicked his actions but pressed harder, seeking more from him; he chose to be gentle, but she had agreed to no such thing. Their kiss went from chaste to chaotic in an instant. Her hands flew up to his chest, grabbing at his shirt to pull him closer. She nipped at his lower lip and then her tongue was dueling with his, trying to defeat him in this one battle where she might have some advantage.

A sudden thrashing in the woods scared them apart, where they stood panting and staring at each other with heated gazes. A plump hare shot out from the underbrush, pausing between them with a quizzical look before darting away. Kate didn't know who started laughing first, but soon both she and Elijah were caught in a fit of hysterics.

This is what happiness feels like, she thought as tears, the good kind, welled in her eyes and her sides ached from mirth. *I'd forgotten.*

"We should get back, Kate," Elijah said finally. "Thank you."

"Yes, we shouldn't tarry," she said, adjusting her frock. She ignored his gratitude, which was too similar to a goodbye for her liking.

As they drew closer to the camp, there was a furor ahead of them, the yells of soldiers and the banshee screams of something that sounded inhuman. As Elijah barreled past her, she realized it was a horse.

They emerged from the trail into a scene of madness. The biggest horse she had ever seen leapt wildly near the Captain's tent. It kicked and bucked, its eyes rolling madly as if it knew not why it behaved so. Soldiers with whips lashed at it, which seemed to spur the horse's fit even more.

"Stop!" Elijah shouted. His booming voice raised the hairs on her neck but was drowned out in the fracas. The group of women who had served breakfast with Kate scattered as the horse charged them — all but Lettie, who stood frozen with fear. The horse reared up, blocking the woman from her view. There was a sickening crack.

"Stop," Elijah said, grabbing at a soldier's arm as he pulled back to release another whip crack. "You're crowding the creature, everyone back away now!"

He approached the frenzied animal, his hands held out before him. Kate recognized the motion: it was the same way he had first approached her.

"It's okay, girl," he said in a soothing voice. "Calm down now, everything will be all right."

The horse backed away from him, eyes still rolling, and it was only then that Kate saw what appeared to be a bundle of rags that had been caught beneath its hooves.

"Lettie," she choked out. She wanted to run to the woman, but Elijah held a staying hand, as if he knew her intentions without even looking at her. He was gazing into the horse's eyes, making comforting noises as he approached. The animal reacted to his calm, stopping in its tracks and staring at him. Its great body was lathered with sweat, and its chest heaved like a bellows, but it didn't move as Elijah stepped up to it and placed a hand on its head.

The horse stamped its hooves and shook its head free and for a horrifying moment Kate thought it would go wild again. Instead, Elijah spoke in a low, soothing voice and placed his hand on the animal's head once more. Slowly, he moved his free hand down to the loose reins, pulling a little. The horse calmly took a step in the direction he pulled, and then whinnied, pressing its face against his shoulder as if seeking comfort.

Whispers of amazement buzzed through the gathered soldiers.

"Come to her now, Kate," Elijah said, and Kate hurried toward Lettie. She already knew from the strange angle of Lettie's neck and the way she lay crumpled that it was too late, but she knelt beside her nonetheless.

"She's done for," one of the soldiers said. "Should we throw her in the pit with the dead prisoners?"

Anger welled up in Kate.

"This woman cooked for you, cleaned your uniforms and your filthy knickers, and that's the respect you show her? A child is motherless now!"

A few of the soldiers looked genuinely upset, but most were excitedly discussing Elijah's handling of Bellamy's horse. Lettie was beneath their concern.

Kate's eyes locked with Elijah's as he stroked the horse's white mane. Another body lay between them; it seemed that death intended to be a bosom companion to them. Part of her wondered if this was the cost of a kiss, the cost of experiencing lust and happiness again after all these years. She'd known that there would be a price to pay for her joy — there always was — but she hadn't expected it to come this soon.

"Mama?" a high-pitched voice called out, and she turned just in time to catch Charlotte in her arms again. This time, Lettie would not be arriving to take the girl away from her.

"Don't look, little one," Kate said as she pressed the girl's head into her neck so she couldn't see the trampled remains. "Your mama has gone away. I'm sorry."

"Can I go with her?" Charlotte asked. She was starting to cry, although she was too young to understand exactly what had passed.

"No," Kate said. Although every part of her fought against it, she knew what she must do. She had vowed never to take on this task again, and it made her ill to even think of it.

"I want to go with Mama," Charlotte hiccupped.

"No, you have to stay here with me," Kate said, feeling as if she were falling into an endless void as she spoke the words. "I'll take care of you now."

CHAPTER 5

ELIJAH HADN'T MEANT to kiss Kate, but after he'd taken that step toward her and closed the space between them, he'd wondered how he could possibly have done anything else. Everything within him shifted hard and fast in her direction as soon as their lips touched, like a horse pulling against the reins with all its might. His chest had pulled tight and every part of him had wanted to know her. Carnally, yes, but in every other way, too. He'd seen the hurt in her eyes, the deep pain that was just as much a part of her as her barbed words. He hadn't pitied her—Kate wasn't the kind of woman who would sit well with that—but he'd been moved all the same.

That the sweetness of their kiss had been chased by bitter sorrow had only galvanized the need for her, the hope for more than any man could rightly expect. Life could end quickly, brutally, and with no warning, but sometimes it could offer you something that gave all the difficulties new meaning.

Kate. Katie. Infuriating and alluring, somber and solid and seemingly made for him. There was no room for a woman like her in his future, but Elijah wanted her all the same.

After the chaos had died down, when he'd seen her clutching Lettie's daughter like a woman lost in an all-encompassing fog, he'd known he couldn't leave her. Something in the woman had laid him low, and although she didn't need his help, he wanted to provide it all the same.

Thus, only one of the prisoners had accepted Bellamy's offer and defected to the British's Colored encampment: Elijah himself. Bellamy had been impressed with his handling of the panicked horse and offered him a position caring for the officers' steeds on the condition that he renounce his ties with the Colonists. It took every ounce of Elijah's strength to endure the hatred of his compatriots in the aftermath of such a treacherous decision.

He'd hoped the British would accept his sham turncoating without question, but it galled that his fellow Patriots so easily fell for his ruse. However, being free to wander the camp had an additional benefit, apart from proximity to Kate: it meant he could cobble together an escape plan for the men. Elijah endured their recriminations—the angry words only made him work faster. A few had already been transported to the prison ships, but Elijah had finally put everything in place to free the others. He could only hope that by doing so, he would regain their trust.

And what about Kate? Can you truly leave her behind?

Elijah felt the warm, humid breath of his latest charge on his neck as he walked forward, paused, and took two steps to the side. He didn't have to look behind him to know that the great nutmeg-colored beast mimicked his footsteps. He'd worked with her for the better part of a week, and he was damned good at what he did. She was already capable of more, much more, but this simple demonstration was for entertainment. A distraction.

Charlotte clapped with delight in Kate's arms, her loss temporarily forgotten. The girl missed her mother, but she was young enough that equine tricks could bring her joy. He wished it was as easy to make Kate smile.

He walked the horse over to Kate and had it bend down on one knee in front of her in an elaborate bow.

"My lady," he said, reverently. "Nutmeg holds you in her highest regard."

The soldiers clapped and laughed, but Kate was looking at the happy little girl in her arms, a frown pulling at her lips.

"Okay, show's over, mates," Elijah said, leading the horse to its pen. The lobsterbacks groaned in disappointment, the same as Master Sutton's children had back on the farm. He glanced at Kate. "I'll walk you back to your tent."

She nodded, a far-away look in her eyes. As soon as he was beside her, she passed Charlotte over and then crossed her arms over her chest.

Charlotte settled against him, babbling as she drifted off into a nap.

"It must be difficult, this sudden responsibility of a child," Elijah said. "I'm sure one of the families in the camp would be willing to take her, if that's what's best for you."

"Do you think I'd purposely abandon this child?" Kate's temper flared, and for a second he had a glimpse of the woman he'd first met. She gave Charlotte's chubby hand a quick squeeze, and then pulled away.

Elijah sighed, not sure he should press the issue. He'd spent most of his free time over the past week with Kate, but that didn't mean she would welcome his meddling. "It's just...I'm worried about you. Sometimes it seems as if you can't stand to touch her."

"Sometimes I can't," she said simply. "Sometimes, she reminds me of something I'd very much like to forget."

The sadness in her voice was enough to undo him. "Is that the same reason why you push me away, too?"

She went rigid beside him, but didn't answer.

"You can talk to me, if you'd like. You've certainly listened to me ramble on over the past week."

She shook her head.

"Kate—"

"I said I want to forget. It's not some mystery you need to solve, Sutton. It's just the story of a headstrong girl who thought love was enough to perform miracles and learned that it wasn't." Her breath hitched and her next words were stilted. "Please don't ask me again."

"I won't."

He reached out and took her hand. He hadn't agreed not to comfort her. He thought she might pull away, but she didn't. After a moment, she sighed and gripped his hand harder, and it was almost as good as their kiss.

They walked on in silence. He realized what they must look like, he and Kate and Charlotte: like a family.

"Maybe you'll feel better after a bite to eat?" He laid Charlotte down in Kate's tent, and then stepped back out. His tent was a distance from hers, on the furthest end of the encampment—the perfect place to strike out at night and survey escape routes. He didn't know if the route he had chosen was the best, or if the sympathetic boatman he had spoken to could be trusted, but the plan was in place. Now he only needed to act. But first...

"Would you like to share supper?" He tried to mask the urgency in his tone, and knew he failed. He couldn't leave without letting her know how he felt—without asking her to come with him when the plan was finally put into action.

"I think I'd better not," she said, sliding past him and into her tent. "Good evening to you, Elijah."

He stood and stared at the flap, stinging at the sound rejection. He'd felt the ardor in her kisses, the way she pulled him closer as if she couldn't get enough of him. And although she'd been reserved in the wake of Lettie's accident, he'd still caught her looking at him with something more than friendship. He had to go to her, had to convince her to join him.

Elijah took a step toward the tent and then shook his head, disgusted with himself and his entitled frustration. Kate wasn't a horse that he could bend to his will, even if he did it through kindness and not violence. She was beautiful and strong, and she'd likely been made to pay for that. He was surely just another man in a long line of them who'd wanted her for their own.

You're...different.

He remembered her words from that first night of his capture, and regretted that he hadn't lived up to them in that moment. Soon, it would be too late to make his amends.

Elijah returned to his tent and flopped onto his sleep roll. After quickly eating some hardtack, he closed his eyes for what felt like seconds but awoke to a stillness that told him hours had passed. It wasn't quiet by any means: crickets chirped loudly, trees susurrated in the wind, and, if he listened very carefully, waves clapped against the distant riverbank. It was time to move.

Elijah crept out of his tent. He wanted to examine the route that led to freedom for him and the remaining prisoners one last time. When the time came, he'd have to act at a moment's notice, and he couldn't lead them astray.

He walked quietly through the trees, hoping the shadows of the night masked his bulky frame. For all that he was large, he moved lightly, but after a few moments he realized he was being followed. Sweat broke out on his brow as his mind raced for some way to evade discovery.

He heard the babbling of a brook and quickly turned toward it. The footsteps followed him, but no one demanded that he come to a halt so he continued. When he reached the brook, he stopped and casually pulled off his shirt. He slid off his boots and began struggling out of his tight breeches. He thought the soldier following him would move on when he saw that Elijah was bathing, but when he dropped his pants to the ground he heard a sharp gasp behind him.

He turned, and some part of his mind knew who it was before his eyes made out her form in the darkness.

"Kate? What are you doing here?" he asked, stepping toward her. A cool breeze reminded him that he was completely nude.

Her eyes were wide in the moonlight. She was silent, although he could hear the faint sound of air passing through her lips as she tried to form words. He should have been cold in the night air, but his body warmed as he took another step toward her. His member thickened against his leg, and he stopped in his tracks.

"Why are you here?" he asked, lowering his hands to shield himself. Her presence wasn't helping, as that which he endeavored to hide grew larger precisely because she was so near. "It's not safe, Kate. What do you think happens to women who stumble upon naked men in the dark woods with no one to interrupt them?"

He didn't mean for the words to sound like a threat, but he was still surprised when they were met by her deep laugh.

"I haven't stumbled upon just any man. You're Elijah Sutton and you wouldn't hurt me," she said. He was heartened by the surety of her tone. The last thing he wanted to do was hurt her, ever. But, in that moment, what he wanted was nothing so gentle as she was used to from him.

"No, I wouldn't. But my thoughts aren't as pure as you might imagine right now."

He expected the words to drive her away, but she began to close the distance between them instead.

"I thought you were running off," she said. "Without saying farewell to me."

Her voice trembled, and now she was near enough he could see the determined expression on her face.

"How did you know I'd left my tent?" he asked. The look in her eye gave him some idea of her answer, and when she reached out and ran her hands over the broad expanse of his chest, he knew he was right.

"I went to your tent because I wanted you to love me," she said. "I know you mean to escape or die trying, no matter what you told Bellamy. Elijah, you're the only man…"

She looked away then, as if she couldn't meet his eye. Elijah wanted to hold her, wanted to stroke her and tell her it was okay, but there was a time for comfort and there was a time for listening. This was the latter.

"I've been touched by many men, but you're the only one I've longed for," she whispered in her lyrical voice. "All of the others took and took. One of the women on the plantation finally taught me how to fight back, and then I was too much trouble to bother with. I got a husband, eventually, but he was so much older, and I never felt this way about him.

"I never felt real pleasure, good pleasure, until you drank from my ladle. Just your hand touching mine made me dizzy, even though I've been caressed all over. When you kissed me… Elijah, I didn't know I could feel like that. And I don't know if I ever will again. I want you to make love to me now."

Elijah's heartbeat resounded in his ears in the silence after her words. The woman he wanted was entrusting him with something more intimate than even her love—her desire. Women gave their hearts away to unworthy men as a matter of course, but confiding the bare truth of one's needs was rare for either sex.

He grabbed the fabric of her cloak and pulled her against his body. He knew she could feel the length of him through her clothing — he'd never been harder in all his life. To ask her if she was sure of her wants would be belittling, so he kissed her instead. His lips trailed across her brow, dragged against the sensitive shell of her ear and lingered there when she shuddered into him. She liked that. Her arms wrapped around him, and the swell of her breasts pushed into his chest, her pebbled nipples scraping pleasurably across his skin.

His hands slid up her back and over her shoulders, mapping her body before cupping her jaw to angle her mouth toward his. This wasn't like the first kiss, gentle and exploratory. His tongue dove into her mouth, assured of its reception, and she met him with the same ferocity. Their bodies swayed and glided, searching for sparks of pleasurable friction. Her mound rubbed over his rigid length, and he groaned into her mouth.

Christ, she feels like heaven, Elijah thought. Every part of him longed for her. The lust that welled up within him was encased in the finest membrane of love, an adoration that hadn't yet hardened to its full strength but would soon be unbreakable.

You must leave this place. And perhaps Kate as well.

The thought of separating from her sent a surge of desperation through him. He needed to touch her, to taste her. He pulled off her cloak and fumbled at her dress, but she moved away from him, efficiently freeing herself and stepping out of the frock.

He stared at her, drank in the beauty of her dark, willowy form before pulling her to him again. He touched her everywhere, hands sliding over her smallish breasts, tucking in at her waist and following the flare of her hips that tapered down to her thighs. He dropped to his knees, resting his face against her firm belly, taking in the smell of soap and Kate's own musky desire. From this close, he could see the striations on her skin where her belly had once stretched with child. He ran his fingertips over the marks, kissing them softly as understanding set in. She'd had a child somewhere along the line, and now she didn't.

His heart ached for her.

"Elijah, please," she groaned. He pulled her down to her knees, too, his mouth searching for hers as he reached behind him to pull his coat beneath them. Their lips were fused when he sat back and she followed, straddling him. The ground was hard, but he ignored the rocky terrain and focused on the soft, sleek woman atop him.

His tongue circled first one nipple, then the other, lips closing around each in turn as she shook with pleasure. He rocked his hips up and his member nudged at her folds. She was damp with desire, and it would have been a simple thing to slide into her warmth. Elijah waited, though. He knew that this was something she must take for herself. He didn't have to wait long. Kate reached down and wrapped her hand around his thick length, hand sliding teasingly up and down his shaft as she slowly took him inside of her. Her other arm went around his neck, fastening her to him as if she were afraid she'd fall.

"Yes," he hissed. "Yes, my dear Katie."

She didn't respond, but her mouth brushed against his forehead and then his cheekbone, brief touches that drove him nearly as mad as the warmth enveloping his cock.

Kate was all tight deliciousness pulsing around his organ. She teased him as she adjusted to his girth, taking him inch by slow inch. Finally, *finally*, he was in her to the hilt, sensation racing down his spine and up his cock as he pulsed into her. His hands went to her hips to support her as he searched for the rhythm that would give her the most pleasure. She threw her head back and gasped, her hips moving in fierce circles to meet his thrusts. She braced herself against his chest, her nails leaving crescents of pleasurable pain as she moved on his cock. Her hands slid up to his shoulders, and her gaze met his.

"Elijah, I never knew," she gasped. "I never knew it could be this good."

Elijah had been maintaining a modicum of control, but that slipped away at her words. Pleasure was blossoming in his body, with something else following on its trail, something that made his chest feel full and warm and overflowing. He began to pump into her fast and hard, driving her toward the sweet completion that was nearly upon him. His grip on her hip tightened, and his tongue lashed at her sensitive breasts as he drove into her.

She broke with a wail, back arching and core clamping tightly around his shaft. Elijah grunted and his climax took him, pulling him down into a vortex of immense pleasure that scoured him from head to toe.

There was the sound of their breathing then, mixing with the scrape of leaves in the wind. She pulled herself up off of him and walked behind him, and he heard the splashing of her cleaning herself in the brook. He gave her a moment of privacy, mostly because he wasn't sure he could speak yet.

"I find myself in quite a quandary," he said as she passed by him to retrieve her dress. His hand darted out to encircle one of her slim ankles. She paused, the moon glinting off of her skin making her look like a dark goddess, unattainable to mortal man. God, he hoped that wasn't so.

"What's that?" she asked in a voice that was softer than her usual strident tone.

"I am determined to leave here, but I'm also determined to have you by my side. The boatman who lives near the Dixon farm has agreed to ferry me and the prisoners I free to Manhattan. There, we can make our way to General Washington. You can come with us. With me."

His heart was brimming with hope after their encounter, but her silence was draining it in quick measure.

"Perhaps if it were just me, but I have Charlotte to think of now," she said in a hollow voice. "I must return to her in case she awakens."

She pulled her leg free and began putting on her dress. Elijah stood heavily, pushing up against the dread and disbelief that held him down, and began dressing as well.

"I know that," he said. "I want to provide for both of you, if you'll let me."

She turned to him with a wounded expression.

"You think that's the first time a man has told me that?" she asked, then made a sound of distaste.

Her question was sharp, the precise whip of a lash by someone who has felt its bite and knows exactly where to strike.

"I'm different from other men, remember?" he joked, trying to keep the pleading tone from his voice.

"One thing is the same: you'll leave me eventually and I'll be left to pick up the pieces," she said, shaking her head. "I cannot value fleeting pleasure over Charlotte's well-being."

"Fleeting?" Elijah felt the word dig into his heart like bird shot. "I care for you. More than you imagine if you think I'd abandon you. Please reconsider."

"You'll be gone by morning, so there's nothing to consider," she said in the flat tone he was learning to hate. He wanted her to snap at him, to show the liveliness he knew existed within her.

"You've misunderstood," he said. "I wasn't planning on leaving tonight. I'll be here in the morning and I'll still want you to come with me. I'll always want you with me, Katie."

She closed her eyes against his words, and a bit of hope flared in his chest. Perhaps she would change her mind. Perhaps —

"It is you who's misunderstood. The remaining Patriots are to be taken to the prison ships on the morrow," she said. Elijah's heart began to hammer in his chest as the full impact of what she was saying hit him. "I overheard a soldier say so this very night, as you performed for them. That is why I wanted you to love me. Whatever plan you have must be enacted now. Goodbye, Elijah."

She turned and rushed off into the night.

Elijah wanted to bellow his anger. He wanted to chase after her and convince her to change her mind. Instead, he quietly ran toward the barn. He had soldiers to free, trampled heart or no.

CHAPTER 6

KATE LAY IN HER TENT, the passing of the night measured by Charlotte's steady breathing beside her. She jumped at every creaking branch, every scurry of a woodland creature, waiting to hear a cry go up that would signal Elijah's doom.

She could still feel his touch. It was branded on her skin, though the man himself was gone.

Gone.

She'd thought she'd known what finality was: a babe dragged from her arms by a river that demanded payment for her foolishness. A husband who climbed up a river bank and left her to drown.

But this was another pain entirely. She knew her child had left this earthly plane, and she vehemently hoped her scoundrel of a husband had as well, but she would never know what had become of Elijah. If he made it to Manhattan, would he be able to find Washington's army? Would he eventually love another woman, hold her in his arms and make her feel like the most special being ever created? Or would he perish during his escape attempt? Would the brightness created every time he smiled be snuffed from this world?

Agony writhed in her at the thought of it. She wanted to go to him, but the last time she had followed her heart...

Oh, please keep Elijah safe. Please hold him in your graces. She prayed to the God of her slave master and to the faded memory of the Gods of her people. And that is when she knew that she had to go to him.

It was neither revelation nor divine inspiration. Kate simply knew that if she loved a man enough to pray for his life twice — she who had given up all belief in a higher power — then she was meant to be at his side.

She grabbed a linen sheet and placed her and Charlotte's few belongings inside. The bag of coins Elijah had scavenged from Trumbull she tucked into the bosom of her dress. Charlotte groaned in annoyance when Kate hefted her up and wrapped an extra length of linen around her to hold her in place against her chest, but she settled into Kate's arms peacefully as they headed out into the night.

As Kate stole toward the woods, there was a ruckus from the direction of the barn. The distant cries of British soldiers rang out in the night. "The prisoners have escaped!"

Candles were being lit in tents in the Colored encampment as the noise woke the sleeping laborers. Kate did not have much time and was grateful that she knew exactly where to go. She'd been dispatched to the Dixon farm several times to pick up laundry supplies. Now, she simply hoped that she could move quickly and quietly enough to get there without detection.

As she hurtled forward through the trees, trying not to jostle the heavy child in her arms, Kate fought back memories of her first flight through the woods. The child she'd carried then had been much lighter, and her husband had toted her few belongings. When he'd abandoned her and the babe in the raging river, she'd well and truly been left with nothing. Only the current pushing her back to shore had saved her because she'd stopped swimming as soon as it became clear that her life's light, her curly-haired girl, had been snatched from her.

Kate shook those thoughts from her head. She tried to fix on something that inspired hope and Elijah's handsome face appeared in her mind. As she hopped over the underbrush, she thought of how magnificent he'd been in the moonlight, all sculpted muscle as he stood by the creek. He was beautiful, and he'd made her feel beautiful too when he loved her as no one ever had.

She let thoughts of Elijah sustain her as she drew up to the banks of the East River...only to see a boat in the distance, headed toward Manhattan Island at full sail. A strong wind blew from behind her, hastening Elijah away from her.

"No," she whispered. Everything in her went cold as she watched it pull farther and farther away. She'd thought to save herself from pain by leaving him before he could leave her, but now she regretted it dearly. She'd prevented him from breaking her heart, but only because she'd done a bloody good job of it herself.

She sank to the ground, Charlotte's weight and her fatigue finally catching up with her. She was unable to pull her gaze from where the boat had faded into the darkness until a hot blast of hay-scented breath snuffled into her ear.

She ducked to her side, shielding Charlotte who squirmed against her chest before groggily whispering, "Nutmeg!"

Kate looked over her shoulder with the thought that she'd been driven to madness by her longing for Elijah. For there he stood, holding the reins to the best trained horse in King George's Army.

"You're supposed to be on the boat," Kate said angrily. She was unsure why she was suddenly so upset, as she had only just been at the edge of despair when she thought him gone. Perhaps that would have been easier than facing him, for now he must know that she well and truly cared for him. What would he do with that knowledge?

"It appears I am not," he said in the kind tone that raised her hackles and made her want to run to him at the same time. The horse whinnied its agreement. "I decided to stay behind in the hopes that a hardheaded woman would eventually succumb to my pleas."

"That hardheaded woman had a moment of softness," Kate said. "She isn't sure she should chance America, but she's willing to take a chance on you."

He was quiet for a long time. When Kate looked at him, she could see his Adam's apple working in his throat.

"If the British find out you had anything to do with the prisoners escaping, they'll kill you," she said quietly. The waves crashed into the shore, their echo raising the hairs on her neck. "And now we're trapped here."

"Do you know how to swim?" he asked, and she was struck by memory of a hard wave crashing over her head, pulling her beneath the cold surface and tumbling her until her arms were pried open. She squeezed Charlotte closer to her.

"Yes," she said. "I certainly can't make it to Manhattan, though, especially not carrying Charlotte."

"Well, you won't have to swim if Nutmeg does her job. This horse is strong and healthy and swims like a fish," Elijah said, handing the horse a slice of apple. It took the fruit delicately between its teeth and huffed happily.

Kate was not happy, though. She was too preoccupied trying to be brave. She was trying to master her fear, but it held her in its icy grip even as her mind battled against it.

"Do you trust me?" Elijah asked.

"No," Kate said immediately, reflexively, but shook her head when she saw the dismay on his face.

"I killed my child, you see," she blurted out, eyes locked on Elijah though she wanted to look away. The words, bottled up for years, came out in a torrent. "My husband told me we had to escape because he was to be sold off. He said the tide would be low and the current gentle, but the river had swelled from rain...others told me not to attempt it, but I scoffed at them because I trusted him. He didn't even try to help us when he made it to the other side, just kept running. I hate him for what he did to me!" She stopped and gulped a breath. She'd never spoken her pain aloud before. "I don't know if I can do this again."

By now, the tears were flowing freely. She rocked Charlotte soothingly, but the child was fast asleep. It was she who needed soothing.

Elijah released the reins and pulled Kate into his arms, wrapping her and her ward in the warmth of his affection. It felt so wonderful to let go, to not hold the grief and shame inside of her, where it poisoned the well of her soul.

"Kate, I will let nothing befall you or Charlotte. I know this is going to be the most frightening thing you've ever done, but I promise you with everything I am that we will make it across that river. There, my men wait for us. There, freedom waits for us. Do you know what they wrote in the Declaration of Independence, the foundation of this new nation of ours?"

At this point she would usually tell him that America was not her home, but looking at the brightness in his eye and hearing the fervor in his tone almost had her convinced. She shook her head.

"It says that we have certain inalienable rights," he said in a voice that was rough with conviction. "Life. Liberty. The pursuit of happiness. They may not be ours just yet, but by God, they will be."

She trembled in his arms as the immensity of his words shook her. Happiness a right? She'd always thought of it as a foolish dream. But this damned Continental of hers was infectious in his enthusiasm.

"I will try, Elijah," she said. Just the thought of it made her want to throw herself onto the safety of the shore and cling, but she turned her back on it instead. "Let us go. Now, before I change my mind."

"My brave Katie," he murmured tenderly, and knowing that he believed her to be so emboldened her to believe it herself.

She pulled away from him and glared out at the great, dark expanse of water ebbing and flowing before her. She had crossed many miles of it on that journey from Africa to America, and she had survived. The water had tried to claim her along with her daughter all those years ago, and it had failed. Let it try again tonight: she would best it. She knew now that love could drag you under, but it could buoy you as well.

She pulled Elijah in for a long, tender kiss before he boosted her up onto the horse. He lifted her skirts up and tied them under Charlotte, to provide some protection from the water and to allow Kate to kick and swim freely if she needed to. He met her gaze as he led Nutmeg toward the rocky beach. Kate's breath quickened as they stepped into the water, as the cold, inky liquid began to lap at her feet and Nutmeg kicked out against the current.

Elijah squeezed her hand before releasing it to paddle beside the horse. His stroke was strong and confident.

"Be not afraid, my love," he said, glancing up at her with hope and something much stronger burning in his eyes.

Kate squeezed her thighs tighter around Nutmeg and set her gaze across the moon-dappled river. She did not know what awaited them when they reached Manhattan Island, but with Elijah at her side she had no doubt that they would make it there.

EPILOGUE

March 1786
Suffolk County, New York

A LOG SNAPPED in the fireplace of the small cabin and Kate's gaze flew from the book perched beside her toward the sound. Her heart started to speed up, and she instinctively moved to run for Charlotte, but she took a deep breath.

The war is over now. I am safe. I am home.

The idea was still novel to her, even three years after the war's end. When they'd made it across the river all those years ago, Kate had expected that her bad luck couldn't be far behind. When Elijah had shown up on his master's doorstep and explained that there was a new provision to their deal—that Mr. Sutton had to shelter Elijah's family while he fought for America's freedom—Kate had thought they'd certainly be turned out into the streets. But she'd spent the war working for Mr. Sutton, whose last remaining slave had taken her chances with the British, and Elijah had eventually returned home when many other men hadn't.

Her small family all had their free papers, and a home, and each other.

Sometimes she wondered what would have come to pass if she'd stayed at the camp and left for Canada, where most of the Black Loyalists had been repatriated. The reports in the paper about the hardships they faced there angered and saddened her. She'd called Elijah naive once, but she could think of no other reason for her surprise. There was no utopia awaiting those who had been pressed into bondage, but there was the hope and happiness they could make for themselves and their people.

She got up and threw more wood on the fire to keep the early spring cold at bay. Elijah and Charlotte would be home soon, and she wanted the house blazing for them.

Elijah had returned from Yorktown in one piece, but his years on the battlefield affected him in other ways. Now the chill seeped into his knees and ankles, settling in with an ache that he grit his teeth against. That didn't stop him from spending his days out with the horses, calling on the surrounding farms, or being active in the Colored community. And even when the pain hit him hard, that didn't stop him from being kind.

There were heavy footfalls in the distance, then the scuffing of boots on the mat outside the door. The heavy wooden rectangle pushed in, got stuck against the jamb, then swung open, and there he was.

Elijah.

Still big and strong after all these years. Still smiling that smile that made her all warm-cheeked and flustered.

Every time he returned home to her, she felt the unconscious fear that he wouldn't drop away, leaving her light and buoyant. She would never lose the dread that her happiness could be snatched away from her; no amount of love and security could pry away the clinging knowledge of experience. But she had learned that living with fear and living *in* fear were two different things. Living in fear meant cutting yourself off from all that might sustain you, and Kate had taken the first step away from that way of life years ago, had let the waves of the East River wash away the anger and hurt that she'd thought could protect her. The change hadn't been easy and was still in progress, but Elijah was still hers and she was still his, so she thought perhaps she hadn't fared too badly.

"Good evening, Mr. Sutton."

He shut the door against the cold and leaned back against it, and from across the room she could feel his gaze raking over her.

"Charlotte's putting up the horses. She insisted she could do it herself," he said, the pride in his voice unmistakable.

"If only that girl paid half as much attention to her needlework." She shook her head, but part of her was proud of their daughter, too. Proud that Charlotte had grown up free, with the choice to shirk her duty and watch Elijah's every move in the horse paddock. In this new country, this new America, maybe one day every little Black girl would have that choice.

"I'd linger in the barn, too, if I knew you were waiting with a pile of sewing to be done." He lifted his chin in the direction of the work piled beside her chair. "Smart girl. Takes after her father."

Kate laughed, and Elijah smiled wide in response. He held his arms out, beckoning her.

"Everything went smoothly?" she asked, stepping into his embrace, letting the comforting, familiar weight of him push away the last of her tension. Elijah was well-known in these parts. Some of the white townsfolk hadn't been thrilled when Mr. Sutton had manumitted his slave and given him land and livestock, as he'd promised, but a good part of their hostility fell away as soon as they had their first horse problem. Apparently, self-interest was a great equalizer amongst men. Still, each time he visited a new farm she worried.

"Yes," he said, pulling her tight against him. He smelled of cold and horse and that light, spicy aroma that couldn't be covered by animal musk or scrubbed away with soap. "They were fine people. Spoke very highly of the new Manumission Society. More importantly, they paid well for my services. We can get those new fabrics you needed for the summer dresses Mrs. Carter wanted made. They're looking to bring in more horses, and they've already requested I come back when they do"

His hands slid to her waist and cinched her there, holding her against him, and the familiar spiral of desire unspooled between her thighs. There was no time for what she wanted, what they both wanted, so just being near him would have to be enough.

"Well, I'm glad the call went better than we expected," she said, leaning into him. She rested her hands on his chest and looked at him, at the gray coming into his beard and the faint lines that creased his face from smiling too often.

"I'm just glad I'm home." The sincerity in his words gave her a pleasant jolt. She knew he wasn't just talking about their modest two room cabin or the belongings they'd scraped together over the years. Not when he was looking at her like that.

She grinned. "Missed me did you?"

"I don't know how many times I have to tell you, Katie," he said. "Every minute I spent away at war, I was longing for you. Every time I leave you now, I feel the same."

Kate felt something in her chest expand almost painfully. She'd been wary of love before Elijah, and still was in many ways. One thing she hadn't realized when she'd stopped trying to evade the emotion was that love wasn't a static thing that you accepted and moved on from — it was wild like the ocean, with dips and swells that would always surprise her. That, even after all this time, a few simple words from Elijah could have joy sprout up in her fast and strong, like a sapling stretching toward the sunlight. She hadn't realized he could make her fall in love with him every day, and that she'd enjoy falling.

She pressed her cheek against his, savoring the scrub of his beard.

"I'd tell you to never leave me, then, but I do enjoy my private reading time," she joked. She had to joke because everything she felt about him was wrapped too tightly around her heart. "But since you missed me so, I'll let you have one kiss before Charlotte returns."

His hand came to her neck to pull her head back, and the heat she saw in his eyes before he kissed her licked higher than the newly stoked flames behind the grate. Then Elijah's mouth was against hers, his lips soft and warm, and his tongue hot and sleek and searching for hers. She felt the love in his kiss and how it nourished her, how it made that sapling grow and branch out until it blotted out the view of her past, and his, shaded them from the cruelties of society, and left them secluded in a world all their own.

"Mama!" The door behind Elijah shook as Charlotte tried to push her way in. "Can you unlatch the door before I catch a chill? Where is Papa?"

Elijah sighed, pressed one more kiss to her lips, and rested his forehead against hers. "Shall we let her in?"

"I don't see why not. I'm quite fond of the girl," she said, stepping away from him. "And of you."

Elijah chuckled and pulled his bulk away from the door, turning to open it as Charlotte's lithe form pranced in on a gust of wind. She kissed Kate on the cheek and then dashed toward the fireplace, holding out her hands toward the warmth.

"Mama, you should have seen the giant stallion on the farm! And they had this sweet little foal that nuzzled my hand! And Papa said maybe, if I did all my sewing and got my letters right, I could go with him again next time!"

"Oh, Char," Kate said. The girl's hair was blown every which way and the hem of her dress was covered in filth. But her eyes were bright and the smile on her face was worth the mess. "Come on, then. Wash up and help me get dinner started. You can tell me all about your day."

Elijah removed his coat and settled into his chair in front of the fire, beside Kate's, after Charlotte dashed off. The girl returned quickly and filled the room with her excited chatter as they prepared the meal. Kate paused in her kneading and took in the scene around her: warm cabin, napping husband, prattling daughter.

I am home.

AUTHOR'S NOTE

When one thinks of the American Revolution, one thinks of powdered wigs and pale skin. In reality, however, African-Americans (both free and enslaved) played a substantial role in the war. The conflict between Elijah and Kate reflects the choices facing Black Americans at the start of the Revolutionary War.

African-American Patriots were a part of the conflict from the very beginning. Crispus Attucks, a Black American, was the first casualty of the war. "Be not afraid!" were the words he supposedly shouted, rallying his fellow Patriots before pandemonium exploded on Boston Common and he was killed. Blacks had already been enlisted as Minutemen in the Massachusetts militia, and many more across the North joined the ranks of the Continental Army. Despite this, in July of 1775 George Washington sent an edict to his recruiters telling them not to enroll "any deserter from the Ministerial army, nor any stroller, negro or vagabond." This ruling was eventually reversed due to lack of manpower.

Meanwhile, in that same year, the Loyalist Lord Dunmore (the Royal Governor of Virginia) sent out a proclamation promising freedom to Blacks, especially the slaves of rebel Patriots, in exchange for service to the Crown. This was actually the first large-scale emancipation of slaves in the United States.

For additional information on this topic, I suggest reading *1776* by David McCullough and *African Americans in the Revolutionary War* by Michael Lee Manning.

If you enjoyed this story and would like to read more of my multicultural historicals, check out *Agnes Moor's Wild Knight*, the story of a Black woman and her Highlander in medieval Scotland, and *Let It Shine*, the story of a Sofie, a 'good girl' who becomes a nonviolent resistor in the Civil Rights movement, and Ivan, the Jewish boxer who teaches her that being bad can be good, too (available in The Brightest Day anthology).

If you'd like to get updates about new releases and exclusive short stories, sign up for my newsletter!

Best,
Alyssa

ABOUT THE AUTHOR

Alyssa Cole is a science editor, pop culture nerd, and romance junkie who lives in the Caribbean and occasionally returns to her fast-paced NYC life. When she's not busy writing, traveling, and learning French, she can be found watching anime with her real-life romance hero or tending to her herd of animals.

Contact her on
@alyssacolelit
Facebook.com/AlyssaColeLit
www.AlyssaCole.com

Made in the USA
Las Vegas, NV
12 September 2021

30158924R00048